My Baby Brother
Has Ten Tiny Toes

Laura Leuck

illustrated by Clara Vulliamy

Albert Whitman & Company

Morton Grove, Illinois

Library of Congress Cataloging-in-Publication Data

Leuck, Laura.
My baby brother has ten tiny toes / written by Laura Leuck;
illustrated by Clara Vulliamy.
p. cm.

Summary: Introduces the numbers one to ten through the nose, eyes,
shoes, and other possessions and body parts of a girl's baby brother.
ISBN 0-8075-5310-7

[1. Babies—Fiction. 2. Brothers and sisters—Fiction.
3. Counting. 4. Stories in rhyme.] I. Vulliamy, Clara, ill. II. Title.
PZ8.3.L565My 1997
[E]—dc20 96-32815
CIP AC

Text copyright © 1997 by Laura Leuck.
Illustrations copyright © 1997 by Clara Vulliamy.
Published in 1997 by Albert Whitman & Company, 6340 Oakton Street,
Morton Grove, Illinois 60053-2723.

Design by Scott Piehl
Text set in AG Book Rounded
Art medium: watercolor

To Matthew and Shane, with love.
—L. L.

For Jack and Martha, with love.
—C. V.

My baby brother
has one tiny nose
that wiggles about
when I tickle his toes.

My baby brother
has two twinkling eyes.
They sparkle and shine
when I show him the skies.

My baby brother
has three silver spoons.
He bangs on his plate
when we sing silly tunes.

My baby brother
has four nifty hats.
His favorite's the one
with the balls and the bats.

My baby brother
has five fluffy bears.
They join us for tea
at my table and chairs.

My baby brother
has six little shoes.

He usually puts on
the pair that I choose.

My baby brother
has seven loud toys.
We play them all day
and make musical noise.

My baby brother
has eight bath time boats.
We fill up the tub
and then watch how they float.

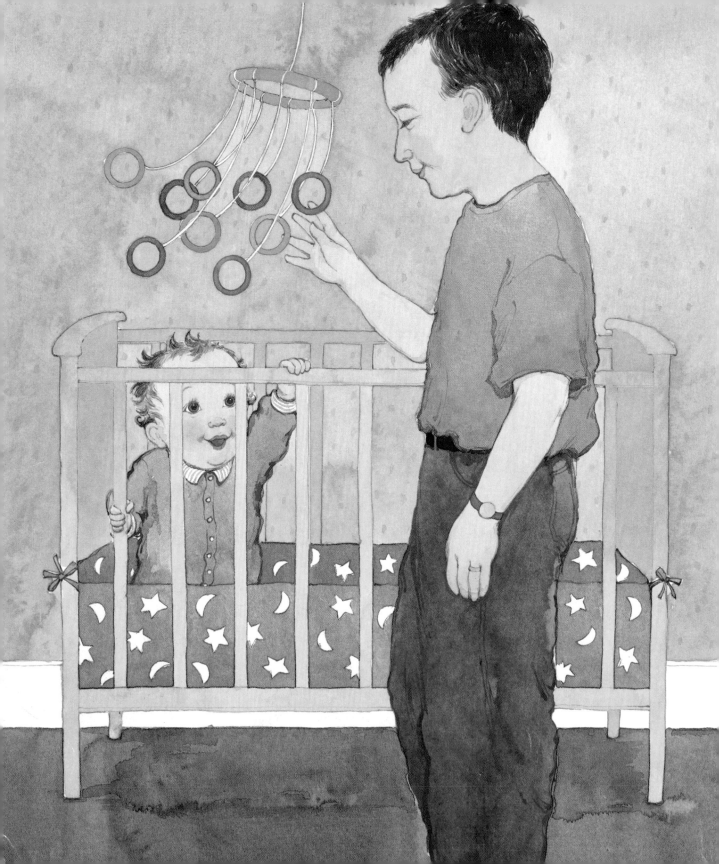

My baby brother
has nine hanging rings.
They jiggle and turn
as he bounces and sings.

My baby brother
has ten tiny toes
that wiggle about
when I tickle his nose.

My baby brother
is smart as can be.
He's lucky to have
a big sister like me!